MR. DALI

MR. PICASSO

MR. MATISSE

EIFFEL TOWER

MR. CHAGALL

For *ma soeur* Gail,
whose love of Paris inspired this book
and who continues to inspire me every day.
−LRL

To Joyce and Malcolm Fletcher,
Peter, and Alice, with love.
−CF

 little bee books

A division of Bonnier Publishing
853 Broadway, New York, New York 10003
Text copyright © 2016 by Linda Ravin Lodding
Illustrations copyright © 2016 by Bonnier Publishing
All rights reserved, including the right of reproduction in whole
or in part in any form. LITTLE BEE BOOKS is a trademark of
Bonnier Publishing Group, and associated colophon
is a trademark of Bonnier Publishing Group.
Manufactured in China LEO 0316
First Edition   10 9 8 7 6 5 4 3 2 1
Library of Congress Cataloging-in-Publication Data is available upon request.
ISBN 978-1-4998-0136-1

littlebeebooks.com
bonnierpublishing.com

PAINTING PEPETTE

written by
LINDA RAVIN LODDING

illustrated by
CLAIRE FLETCHER

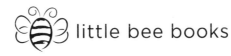 little bee books

Josette Bobette and her rabbit, Pepette,
lived at #9 Rue Laffette, Paris.

Josette adored Pepette and took her everywhere.

But their favorite thing to do was cuddle on
the window seat in the Bobette's great room.

This great room was filled with fine art.
There was a portrait of Josette's mother.
There were the paintings of grand-mère and grand-père.

There were the paintings of
the petite Bobettes—Jeanette, Juliette, and Josette.
There was even a portrait of their schnoodle, Frizette.

One day, Josette noticed something strange.
There was no portrait of **Pepette**!

"We must find an artist to paint your portrait," said Josette.

"And it has to be special—just like you!"

So the two friends set off to Montmartre where the best artists in Paris painted.

Easels filled the square amid the hustle and bustle
of people rushing here, there, and everywhere.

As soon as they turned the corner, a man
in a sailor-striped shirt stopped them.

"THOSE EARS!" he cried.

"Never have I seen such
majestic ears. I *must* paint
this rabbit's portrait!"

Josette noticed Pepette blushing.
Her ears had never been called "majestic" before.
"*Magnifique!*" said Josette. "We are looking for an artist."

The painter propped open his easel and filled his canvas with not one, but *two* button noses, and *three* rabbit ears! When he finished, he waved his paintbrush in the air and declared his painting a "masterpiece"!

"What do you think?" he asked.

"It's nice," said Josette.
"It's just that Pepette has
only one nose and two ears."

And Pepette had to agree.

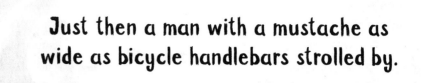

Just then a man with a mustache as wide as bicycle handlebars strolled by.

"What a divine creature!" he said,
twirling the ends of her whiskers.

"Please, I *must* paint the very
essence of her rabbitness!"

The man painted a most unusual portrait.
"You like?" asked the painter, motioning to his canvas.

Josette stood back.
"It's imaginative," she said, trying
to find just the right words.
"But you painted Pepette quite, well, droopy."

And Pepette had to agree.

Moments later another painter wandered by.
He stopped in his tracks when he spotted **Pepette**.

"That nose! Like a faint star
twinkling in a misty, velvet night...."

As he bowed to Josette, a shock of black curls
flopped over one eye.
"May I paint your friend? My easel is
across the square."

"Pepette would like that!" said Josette.
*Certainly this artist would paint
just the right portrait,* she thought.

Pepette and Josette hopped through the square
until they reached the painter's easel.

More and more people gathered around and looked on
as he painted a rabbit . . . flying through the clouds!

When he finished, he admired his painting.
"One of my best works!"

"I like the clouds," said Josette. "But Pepette
doesn't like to fly. She's scared of heights."

And Pepette had to agree.

"**THAT RABBIT!**" said another painter.

He peered at Pepette through his round spectacles.
"What a colorful lady—balloon blue,
pansy pink, and radish red!"

Was he talking about Pepette?
wondered Josette.

"May I have the honor of showing
the world her colors?"

Josette nodded. She was, after all, quite curious.

When the painter finished, he wiped his brow
and revealed his work to Josette.

"Ta-da!"

The canvas was filled with splashes, dashes,
and dots of bright color.
Josette considered the painting.
"It's awfully colorful. But Pepette isn't pink."

"Ah, yes," he said.
"But through art we
can see the world
any way we want."

The sun was setting on Paris, and Josette knew it was time to head home.

"Merci," she said to the artists.
"It's been lovely meeting you."

And **Pepette** had to agree.

That evening, at #9 Rue Laffette in Paris,
Josette and Pepette cuddled on the window seat
in the great room.

Josette sighed. She had hoped that Pepette could have
a portrait that showed her wonderfulness—with her
soft gray ears that listened to her when she was sad,
with her heart-shaped nose that twitched when she was
thinking, and with her soft arms that held her tight.

She had so wanted Pepette to have the perfect portrait.

Suddenly, Josette realized what she had to do....

And she painted the perfect portrait!
It was special—just like Pepette.

And Pepette had to agree.

Author's Note

Paris in the 1920s was an exciting and creative city. Many artists—as well as writers, musicians, and fashion designers—flocked to Paris to work on their craft. While Josette and Pepette are fictional characters, the artists whom Pepette inspires are based on real artists living and working in Paris at that time: Pablo Picasso, Salvador Dalí, Marc Chagall, and Henri Matisse.

Today, Montmartre is still an artsy quarter, but long gone are the days when this area was home to some of the world's most renowned artists. Yet, if you use your imagination, you might still see those artists dart along the cobblestone streets, pitch their easels to capture the warm Parisian light, and maybe, just maybe, spot a girl and her beloved rabbit.

PAINTING
PEPETTE
MUSE OF PARIS